GEOGRAPHY

Name......
class......

MATH

POETRY

Name......
class......

ORGANIC

Honey

Jam

For the Dell family: Andy, Sylvia,
Alastair, Kathryn, Olivia, and Georgie,
who made a new family—M.H.

For Jessie, Lola, Lenny, and Lucie Lorne—R.A.

DIAL BOOKS FOR YOUNG READERS
A division of Penguin Young Readers Group
Published by The Penguin Group • Penguin Group (USA) Inc. • 375 Hudson Street, New York, NY
10014, U.S.A. • Penguin Group (Canada), 90 Eglinton Avenue East, Suite 700, Toronto, Ontario,
Canada M4P 2Y3 (a division of Pearson Penguin Canada Inc.) • Penguin Books Ltd, 80 Strand,
London WC2R 0RL, England • Penguin Ireland, 25 St. Stephen's Green, Dublin 2, Ireland (a divi-
sion of Penguin Books Ltd) • Penguin Group (Australia), 250 Camberwell Road, Camberwell,
Victoria 3124, Australia (a division of Pearson Australia Group Pty Ltd) • Penguin Books India Pvt
Ltd, 11 Community Centre, Panchsheel Park, New Delhi - 110 017, India • Penguin Group (NZ),
67 Apollo Drive, Rosedale, North Shore 0632, New Zealand (a division of Pearson New Zealand
Ltd) • Penguin Books (South Africa) (Pty) Ltd, 24 Sturdee Avenue, Rosebank, Johannesburg 2196,
South Africa • Penguin Books Ltd, Registered Offices: 80 Strand, London WC2R 0RL, England

First published in the United States 2011 by Dial Books for Young Readers

First published in Great Britain in 2010
by Janetta Otter-Barry Books,
Frances Lincoln Children's Books,
4 Torriano Mews, Torriano Avenue,
London NW5 2RZ
www.franceslincoln.com

Text copyright © 2010 by Mary Hoffman
Pictures copyright © 2010 by Ros Asquith

Library of Congress Cataloging-in-Publication Data
is available upon request

Illustrated with watercolors

The Great Big Book of Families

Can you find me on every spread, and figure out what my name is?

by Mary Hoffman
pictures by Ros Asquith

Dial Books for Young Readers ✹ an imprint of Penguin Group (USA) Inc.

Once upon a time, most families in books looked like this:

One daddy,   one mommy,   one little boy,   one little girl,

But in real life, families come in all sorts of shapes and sizes.

one dog, and one cat.

In this book are a lot of families living
in different ways. Perhaps there's one
that looks like yours?

FAMILIES

Lots of children live with their mommy and daddy,

but lots of others live
with just their daddy

or just their mommy.

Some live with their grandma and grandpa.

The Great Big Book of Families

Some children have two mommies or two daddies.

And some are adopted or live with foster families.

WHO'S IN YOUR FAMILY?

Some people have lots of brothers and sisters . . .

great-GRANNY JANE · GRANNY ESME · GRAMPA BILL · granma SUZIE · granpa JOE · great-granMA Evelyn

AUNty JANE · Aunty FLO · uncle BOB · UNCLE AbdUL · AUNty Amy · Sister MIA · AUNty SAdie

My Family

and uncles and aunties . . .

and cousins . . .

and grandmas and grandpas.
And even great-grandmas
and great-grandpas.

But some people have really
small families. You can be a
family with just two people.

HOMES

People live in all sorts
of homes . . .

Some small families live in big houses.
And some big families live in tiny apartments.

And some people can't find
anywhere to live.

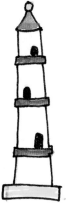

SCHOOL

Most children go to school.

But some are homeschooled.

And some just won't go to school.

Others are too young to go to school.

JOBS

In some families everyone has a job.

In others only one person goes to work.

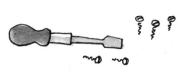

Some parents work from home.

And some can't get
a job at all.

HOLiDAYS

Some families go on exotic vacations,

and some stay closer to home.

Some visit family in other countries.

You don't need to pack EVERYTHING

And others go on day trips.

Not all families
can afford a vacation.
But most people
get some time off
from work. Even a
weekend at home can
be a little vacation.

FOOD

AIKEN DRUM — FINE MEATS SINCE 1896

TOM the PIPER'S SON TAKE-OUT

MENU

Miss Muffet

Some moms or dads
are great cooks . . .

Others prefer to buy
ready-made meals.

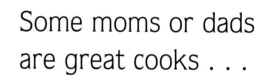

BURGERS 4 US

Jam

Most families get their food
from shops or markets.

But some people grow their own.

CLOTHES

Some children get
new clothes.

Others have hand-me-downs . . .
Or their clothes come from thrift stores.

Are you an Elf?

No. A SOCK

COSTUME PARTY

Some families dress up for special occasions.

But some like to wear
jeans all the time.

And some dress any
way they please.

PETS

Some people believe their pets
are members of their family.

And some pets think they're very
important family members.

Some people even
look like their pets.

Is a teddy
a pet?

Some families can't have pets—but it doesn't stop them from dreaming . . .

And there are ways that every family can have a pet of some sort.

Am I a pet?

CAT

DOG

SNAIL RACE

Birthdays are fun, but some families
make more fuss about them
than others.

And then there is Christmas, Divali, Eid, Hanukkah, Weddings, Christenings, Kwanzaa, Bar and Bat Mitzvahs, Chinese New Year . . .

Whatever you celebrate in your family, there are usually some special traditions.

What are we celebrating?

EVERYTHING!

HOBBIES

In some families everyone has the same hobby.

In others, everyone likes doing different things . . .

TRANSPORTATION

Some families walk everywhere—
to the store, to school,
to the doctor . . .

Others get around in big cars . . .

Or on bicycles . . .

Or riding something else . . .

FEELINGS

In some families everyone shares their feelings.

Other people are more shy. Or perhaps they just like to keep their feelings to themselves.

PRIVATE

Sometimes not everyone in the family feels the same way about things.

And feelings can change quickly.

Have you ever tried to make a family tree?

Sometimes you don't have to go back far to find bits of family who have come from other countries.

And if your mom or dad lives with a new partner,

you might have to make a whole new set of branches.

So families can be big, small, happy, sad,
rich, poor, loud, quiet, mad, good-tempered,
worried, or happy-go-lucky.

Most families are all of these
things some of the time.

What's *yours* like
today?